To my big brother Jacob. I copied you a lot growing up —
more out of competitiveness than admiration, I suspect.

First US edition 2022

Published in 2020
by Berbay Publishing Pty Ltd
PO Box 133 Kew East
Victoria 3102 Australia

Text and illustrations © Gabriel Evans

The moral right of the author and illustrator has been asserted.

Publisher: Nancy Conescu
Designer: John Canty
Printed by Everbest Printing in China

Cataloguing-in-publication data is available
from the National Library of Australia
catalogue.nla.gov.au

ISBN 978-1-922610-44-7
Visit our catalogue at berbaybooks.com

NORTON and the BEAR

GABRIEL EVANS

BERBAY
PUBLISHING

Norton liked to dress differently.

It made him feel unique.

One day he found a sweater.
It was very woolly and warm.

Not a single person in the street had a sweater quite like it.

Norton felt good.

He felt exceptionally unique.

Oh, my! What a lovely sweater!

Quality knitting.

Exquisite pattern.

I must get one just like it.

Look! We match!

Norton was horrified.
He walked quickly away
from the bear.

People would think they
were identical.

He needed to look
different — fast!

Norton chose the
beige scarf.

He felt unique again.

Norton relaxed. The birds were singing.
The sun was shining. Most of all, everyone
around him was dressed differently.

Oh my goodness!

That scarf is the perfect accessory for this sweater. I must get one.

We look so similar! We're like identical twins!

Norton ran from
that annoying bear.

And hid.

Then ran
some more.

And hid.

Then disguised himself and went into a hat shop.

Norton tried every single hat on.

He decided on the green hat. It was the only one
in stock. The bear wouldn't be able to copy him.

Norton left the shop, once more feeling unique.

Yoo hoo!

Norton panicked.
That dratted bear.

He had to look different fast!
He bought socks

Socks over boots?
What a fabulous idea.

Norton stuck a flower in his hat.

Splendid! This adds a touch of
floral sophistication.

Norton shoved a stick
in his sweater.

Now this is a
fashion statement.

Look at us. We're so similar.
I don't know where you end
and I begin. Haha!

Stop copying me!

This is me.
Not you.
I don't want you copying me.
This is MY style.
F-I-N-D Y-O-U-R O-W-N!

I'm sorry you don't appreciate me admiring you. I will endeavor to find my own style.

Good day, sir.

The sun was warm, the birds were singing,
and Norton felt BAD.

Ahem!

I'm not sure if you
recognize me.

This is my cape.
It's my new style.

Norton really, REALLY liked the cape.
He wanted one very much.

I got one for you too.
If you'd like?

Norton decided that wearing the same clothes didn't matter so much.

Let me buy you coffee.

I prefer tea.

And even if they looked identical,
they were still very different.